CoCk-a-dOoDle-Poo!

Steve Smallman

Florence Weiser

LITTLE TIGER
LONDON

Down on the farm there's a **terrible pong**.
(Well, the animals are pooing there all day long!)

Splat!

What's that?

It's a **big** cow pat,

And
the sheep
pop
pellets
out –
rat-a-tat-a-tat!

Pig keeps **plopping** like he's never ever stopping,
And you'd better stand clear
when a horse poo's **dropping!**

Farmer Jill says,
"What you have to understand
Is it might **pong** a bit
but it's **good for the land!**"

But it wasn't so good for
the chickens on the ground,

Dodging bits of **doo-doo** **flying** **all around!**

"Oh, I wish I could fly where the air is clear," groaned Rooster.

"**The pong's too strong** down here!"

One day, Jill came back from the city
With a new hair cut - she looked so **pretty!**

Then somebody cried out,

"CoCk-a- dOoDle-
doo- dOO!"

And plopped on the top
of her nice
new hairdo!

She looked at the animals and she said,
"Who did a doO-dOo on my head?"

Horse said, "I heard 'CoCk-a-dOoDle-doo-doO!'"

"Rooster!" Sheep cried.
"That's what **you** do!"

"Well, it can't be **him!**"
said Hen with a smirk,
"Everybody knows that
his wings don't work.

"Chickens can run,
and flap, and JUMP!

But we can't fly high because
we're just too
plump!"

Jill shampooed
the POO from her hair,

And cried,
"What's happened
to my
UNDERWEAR?

I left my knickers on the line to dry,
So where did they go to?
Pants can't fly!"

It shot

Rooster was hiding,
he felt really bad,
He hadn't meant to doo-doo
on the farmer but he had.

First he'd pinched her **knickers**
and he'd pulled out the elastic,

To make a **rooster**
booster
catapult
(it was fantastic!).

him up into the sky,

he flew a loOp-the-loOp,
He cried out, "CoCk-a-dOoDle-dOo!"

and then he did a poop!

"From now on," he decided,
"I will only fly at night,
In case I have another little
accident in flight!"

So he waited till the **moon** came out
but by its light he saw,
A hungry fox was sneaking
to the
creaking
hen house
door!

Rooster put his goggles on
and shouted, "Time to fly!"

He catapulted off the roof and up into the sky.

"I'll save you, hens!" he cried,
and Fox laughed,
"Really? What can you do?"

"Funny you should ask,"
said Rooster.

"CoCk-a-
dOoDle-dOo-
doO!"

Everyone was woken by the sound
of Rooster CROWING!
So much poop was falling that
they thought it must be snowing!

The poor old fox was **flattened**
by the massive

POOP attACK.

He ran away and Rooster cried,
"Clear off and don't
come back!"

"You've saved the day!" cheered Farmer Jill.
"But I don't understand,
However did you fly so high?
However will you land?"

But Rooster wasn't worried.
No, he couldn't give a hoot.

The farmer's
frilly knickers
made . . .

. . . a perfect parachute!

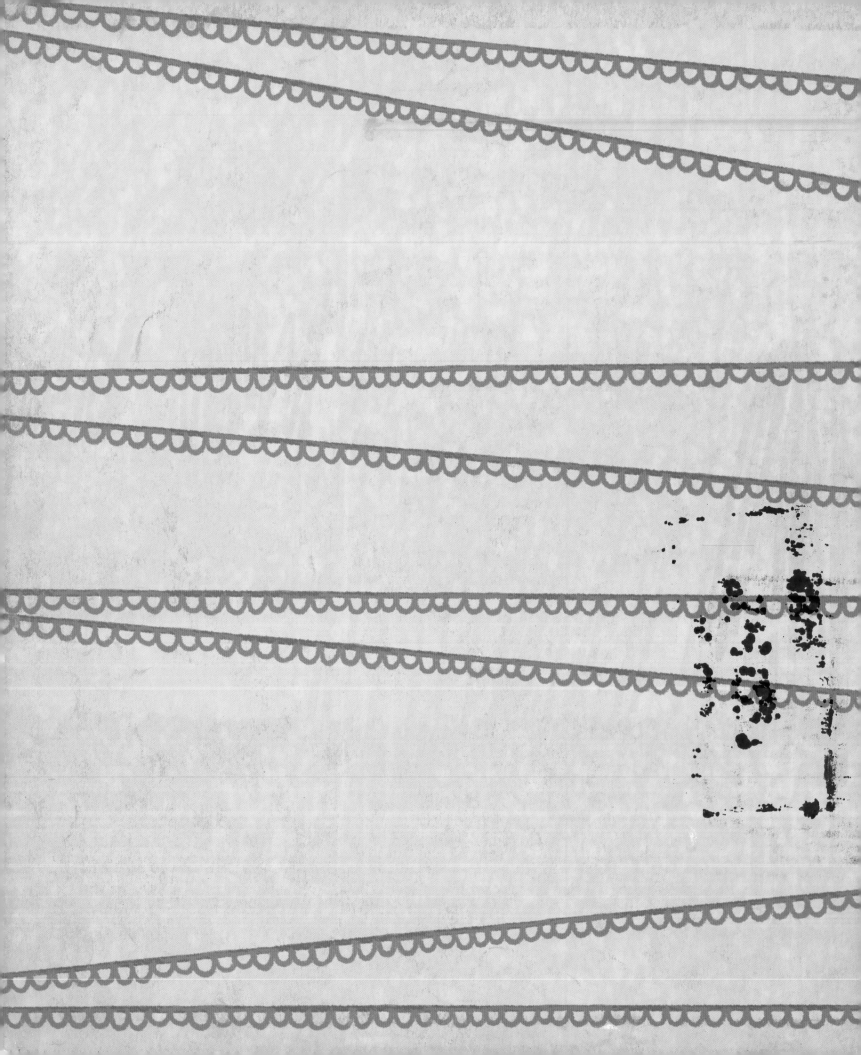